OH NO, BOBO! YOU'RE IN TROUBLE

by **PHIL GOSIER**

ROARING BROOK PRESS / New York

Library of Congress Control Number: 2018944878
ISBN: 978-1-250-17683-7

Our books may be purchased in bulk for promotional, educational, or business use. Please contact your
local bookseller or the Macmillan Corporate and Premium Sales Department at (800) 221-7945 ext. 5442
or by e-mail at MacmillanSpecialMarkets@macmillan.com.

First edition, 2019
Printed in China by RR Donnelley Asia Printing Solutions Ltd., Dongguan City, Guangdong Province

1 3 5 7 9 10 8 6 4 2

For Ethan

Sneak!
Sneak!

Click!

Click!

OooOOOoooh!

Click! Click. Click! Click. Click! Click.

Click-a
click-a-click-
CLICK!

Cluk!

Clik-cluk.
Clik-cluk.

Hmm.

Look! I can FIX it!

Poke!
Poke!
Poke!

SPROING!

GASP!

You broke it even MORE!

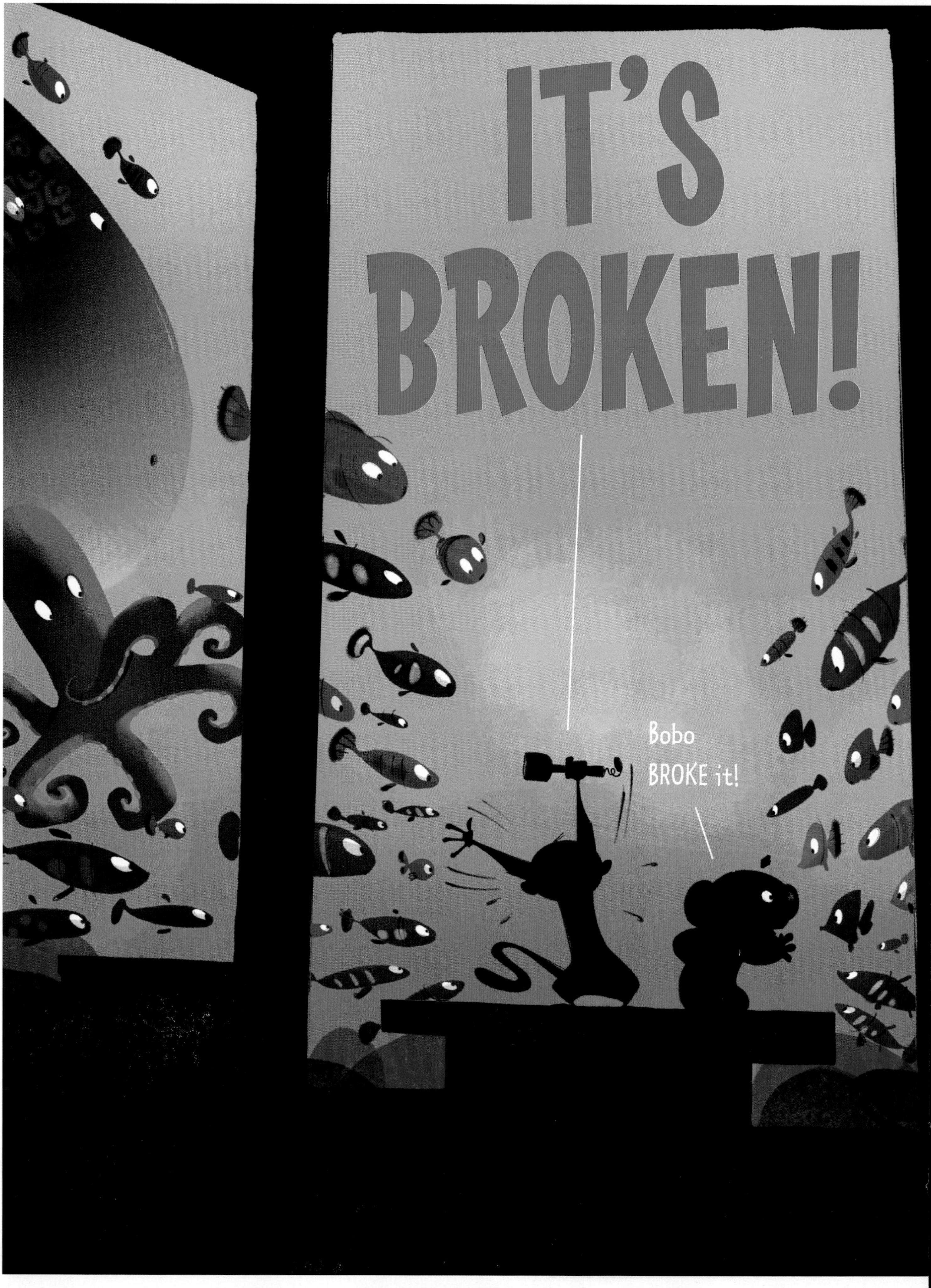
IT'S BROKEN!
Bobo BROKE it!

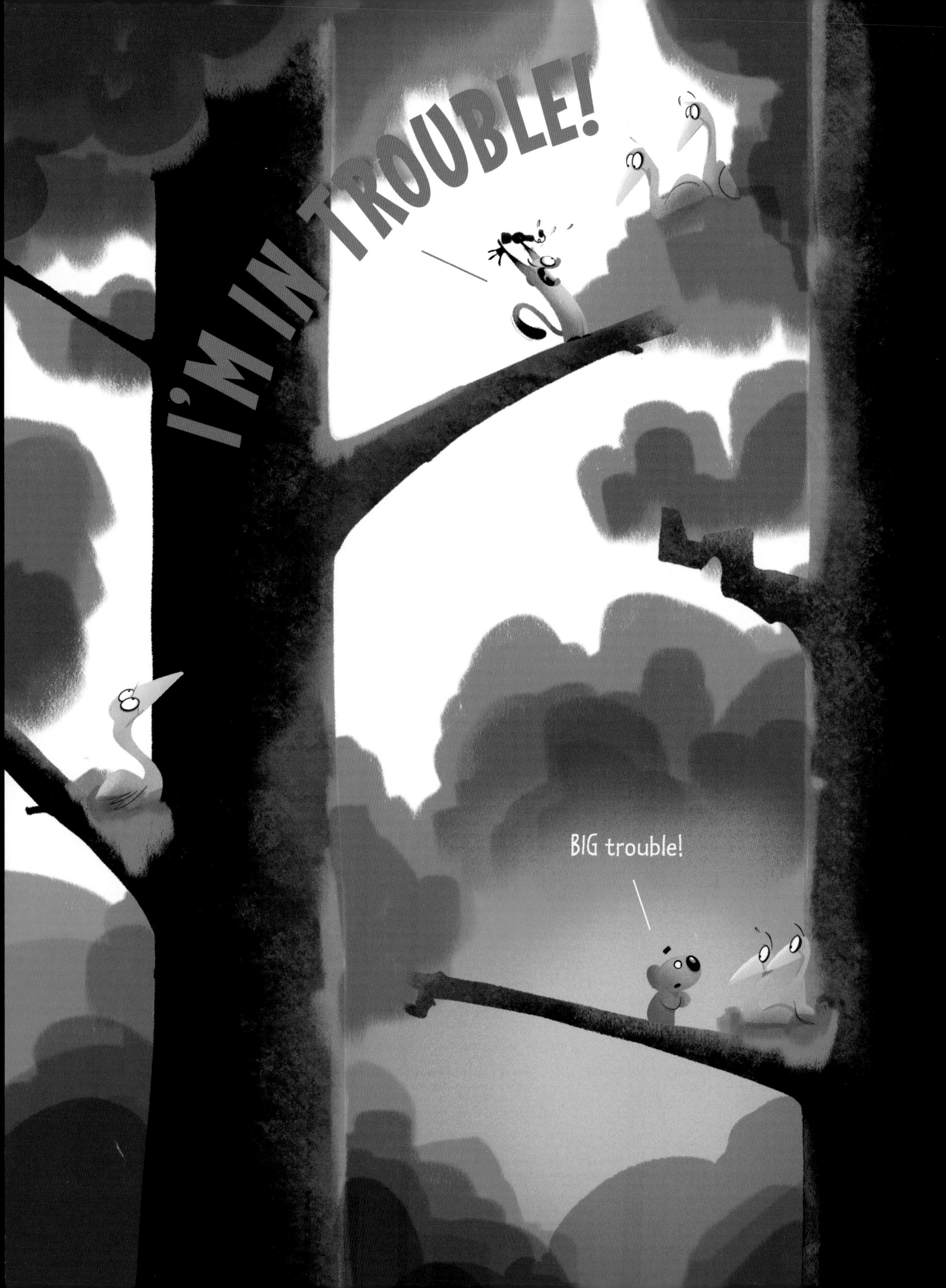
I'M IN TROUBLE!
BIG trouble!

Bobo BROKE the zookeeper's flashlight.

FIFI IS THE GREATEST!
AND SHE'S
SUPER SMART
AND VERY
PRETTY!!

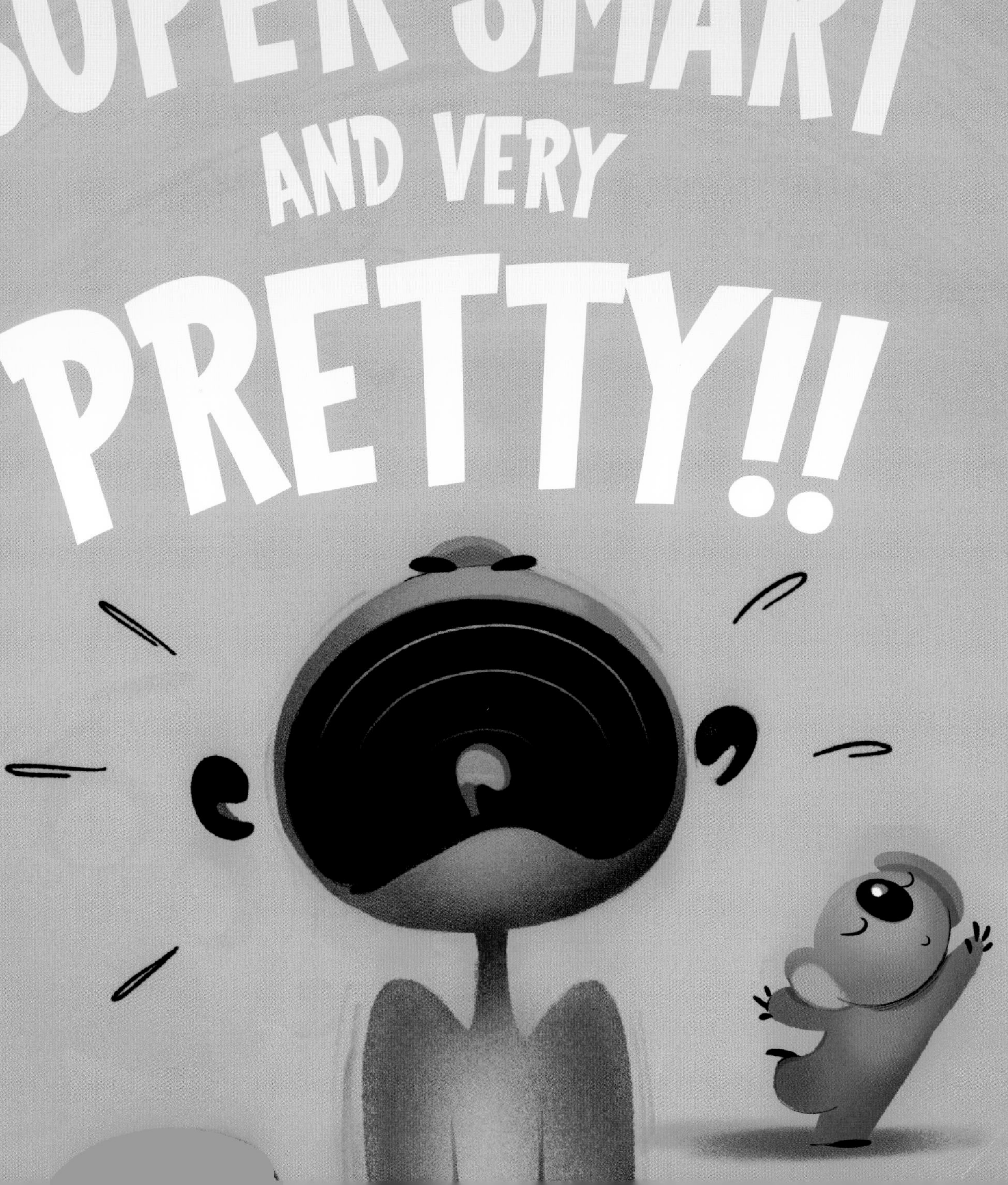

Okay. Calm down. I won't tell.

You won't??

I guess not.
But I can't promise that
THEY won't tell.

Are you going to tell?

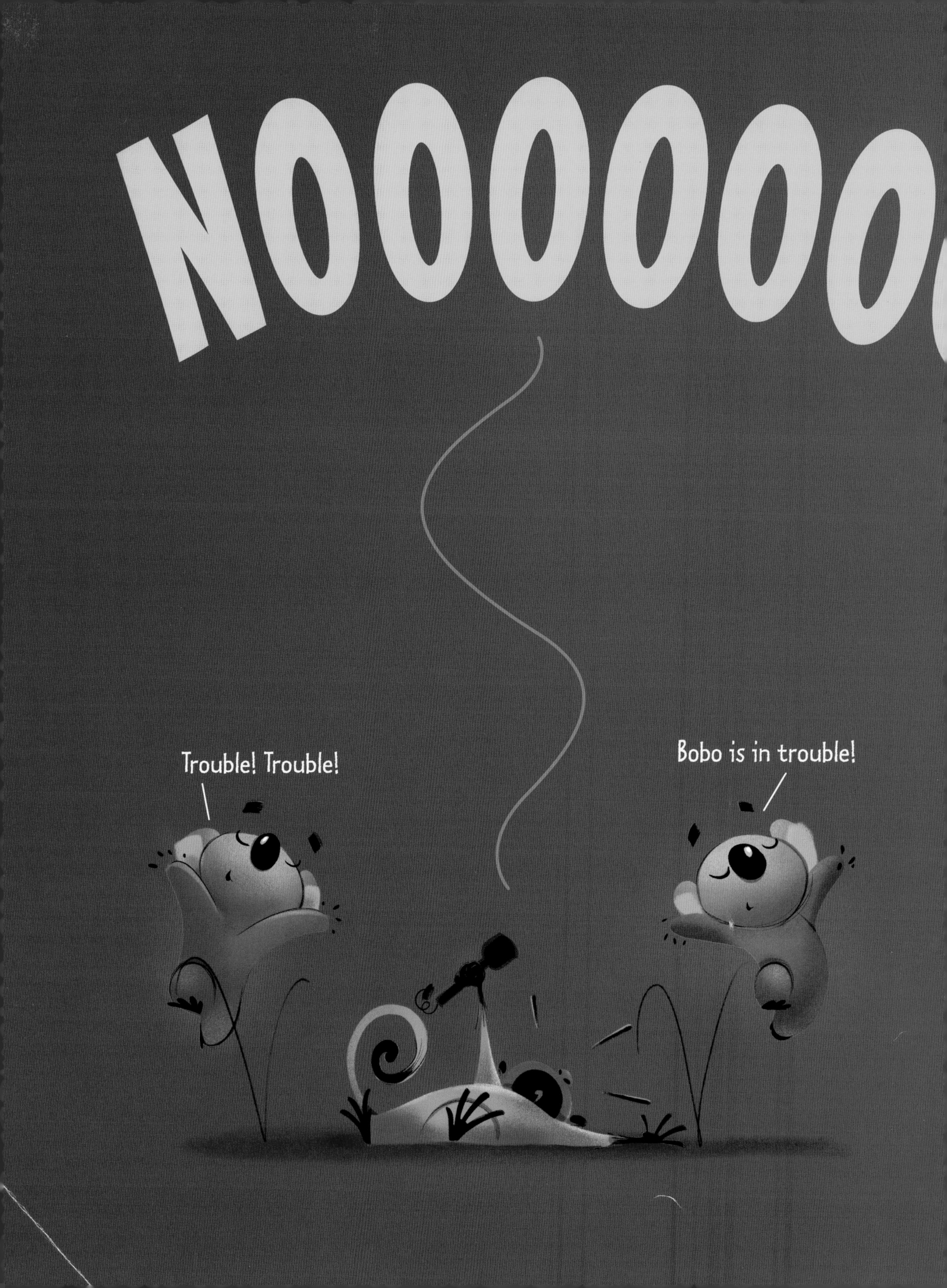
NOOOOOO
Trouble! Trouble!
Bobo is in trouble!

Oh, THERE it is!

Hmm. Looks like it needs new batteries.

Oh.
It was just the batteries.

NOW YOU'RE IN TROUBLE!!